It's a spring Day

Mickie Fosina

Illustrations by: Susan Berger

To order additional copies of this book, contact:
Xlibris
1-888-795-4274
www.Xlibris.com
Orders@Xlibris.com

Dedication

Thank You,
To my husband Joe, for all your support
in seeing me through this project.
It is only because of you that I am
able to have this published.

Thank You
To my niece Diane DeLuca
for all your direction and guidance
in the development of this book

Thank You
To Susan Berger, my new friend
for your beautiful illustrations
that made my script into a
beautiful book

It's a Spring Day!!

I woke up this morning and took a breath of fresh air.
I knew today that spring would be here.

"Good Morning, Amy
you have got to get up."

"It's time for school,
up, up, up" I heard Mother say

Eat your breakfast
and be on your way.

It's a bright and sunny wonderful...
SPRING DAY!!!

So I gathered my books
took my sweater off the hook.

Called my sisters, Katt and Kris
and said "How do I look?"

With blonde hair in pigtails
and polish on my nails

I was ready to go to the
bus stop today

To begin to celebrate this
wonderful...

SPRING DAY!!!

we wait on the corner for
the big yellow bus

that takes us to school
without any fuss.

The air is so fresh and the
trees turning green,

flowers blooming in
gardens it seems like a dream.

School windows are opened
there is a nice cool breeze
our teacher calls out
"Let's start our lessons, please.

"I pledge allegiance to the flag
of the United States of America
and to the Republic for which it
stands one Nation, under God,
indivisible with Liberty and Justice
for all."

"Good morning class" our teacher said
looking out the window with a tilt of her head.

The sky is so blue and we are all here today
to learn and celebrate this beautiful...

SPRING DAY!!!

Let us think of things that make
spring so much fun.

Jacqueline drew a picture of our
school bus and the sun.

Morgan thought more of flying a kite on the run.

When Tori was asked,
she couldn't think of one.

So Stephanie said, "Let's go outside and look around, I'm sure some great spring things can be found.

We saw little purple flowers peaking through the ground.

We saw clovers in the grass and robins in the trees.

We saw buds on the trees and the smell of new leaves.

Oh, today is a warm wonderful...

SPRING DAY!!!

It is late in the day, friends home from
school and at play.

olivia looked in the sky
and saw the clouds rolling by.
She said "it looks like a rain storm is coming."

So, Julia and the girls picked up the toys and
put them away.
She said " and now we will all go inside and play."

As they ran in the house,

we heard the girls say...

"but that's okay"!!

we just had...

A HAPPY SPRING DAY!!!

Printed in the United States
by Baker & Taylor Publisher Services